The Knight of the Lion

The Knight
of the Lion

retold by CONSTANCE HIEATT

illustrated by JOSEPH LOW

Thomas Y. Crowell Company · *New York*

for
LARS

Retold by Constance Hieatt

SIR GAWAIN AND THE GREEN KNIGHT

THE KNIGHT OF THE LION

Contents

1 : THE ENCHANTED SPRING   1

2 : THE RING OF INVISIBILITY   11

3 : THE RING OF SAFETY   20

4 : THE LION AND THE DRAGON   29

5 : THE GIANT HARPIN   38

6 : THE KNIGHT OF THE LION   45

7 : YWAIN AND GAWAIN   56

8 : THE GUARDIAN OF THE SPRING   65

Preface

In retelling the story of Ywain and his lion for a youthful modern audience, I have worked as the medieval storytellers did before me: I have taken some details from one version, some from another, and some from entirely different tales. The result is a story which is, in one sense, entirely my own, but in another, a retelling in the traditional way of a traditional tale.

The original version of this story was written in twelfth-century France by a poet named Chrétien de Troyes, who called it Le Chevalier au Lion. In writing his great romance, Chrétien combined the ancient story of the grateful lion, and many other motifs from other sources, with a story about a magic fountain, or spring, and the lady of the fountain. This story had, apparently, already been associated with a Welsh hero named Owain (modern Owen). Chrétien called his hero Yvain; later editors usually spell it Ivain.

Chrétien's romance was enormously popular, and in the next two centuries a number of adaptations were written in other languages. These include the German Iwein, by Hartmann von Aue; the Old Norse Ivents Saga; and the Middle English Ywain and Gawain. Each of the adapters changed the story in one way or another to suit his particular audience.

I have tried, then, to follow their example.

1: The Enchanted Spring

IN THE DAYS when King Arthur ruled over Britain, the knights and ladies of the land gathered at his court in the spring on the Feast of Pentecost. There they made merry together, jousting and feasting, singing and dancing. But most of all they loved to exchange tales of strange marvels and knightly adventure.

One day in this festive season, while Arthur and his queen rested in their chamber, a group of noble knights kept guard outside their door. Sir Gawain was there, and Sir Kay, and the two cousins Sir Ywain and Sir Calogrant. The others all listened intently as Calogrant told them a wonderful story. Queen Guinevere heard, and came from her room to hear the better. Silently she sat down among

1

them, for she did not wish to interrupt. The knights were so intent on the tale that none but the storyteller noticed that she had come.

Then Calogrant rose to his feet at once. Now Sir Kay could not bear to have anyone appear a better or more courteous knight than himself. "By my soul," said he, "you show great skill in leaping, if in nothing else! Do you think you can put us to shame like that? Why, we would all have risen as gladly as you if we had seen the queen coming."

"For shame, Sir Kay," said the queen. "It is not good to speak to your comrades so."

"He has deceived you, lady," said Kay, "if you think he excels us in courtesy. We know our manners as well as he. But let us not lose by your company, madame. Pray you that he may go on with his tale."

"Good Sir Calogrant," said the queen, "please tell us your story, as you began. You should not heed Sir Kay's sharp tongue."

"Dear lady," said Calogrant, "for your sake alone I will tell my tale. As for Sir Kay, though I count his insults no worse than the bites of a gadfly, I would not wish to show him any favor. But you, my queen, I cannot refuse.

"Listen, then, for what I tell you is true. It was seven years since that I rode through a great forest in search of adventure. There one day I found a clearing full of fearful wild beasts—leopards, lions, bulls, and bears; their roaring and howling was horrible to hear. As I started to draw back in terror, I saw a strange creature sitting there with a great, knobbed club in his hand. His ears were like those of an elephant, his eyes like those of an owl, his nose like a cat's, and his yellow teeth like the tusks of a wild boar. Matted black hair hung over his hunched back and his beard fell to his waist.

2

"He stood up when he saw me, leaning on his club, and I saw that he was a giant—at least seventeen feet tall. I made ready to defend myself, but he made no move and spoke not a word until at last I said, 'What manner of man may you be?' He answered, 'I am the keeper of these wild beasts.' 'How can that be?' I asked. 'Surely no man, no matter how strong or how large, could handle such beasts as these unless they be caged or in chains.' 'Nevertheless,' replied the giant, 'none shall come near you or move from this grove unless I permit it. No beast here is so bold that he dares to disobey me, nor is there any that will not come to my command. But now as for you, sir, who, indeed, are you, and what do you seek in this forest?'

"I answered that I was a knight-errant, seeking adventures where I might gain fame. 'And I pray you, friend,' I said, 'to counsel me where I may find some venture to test my skill.'

" 'Little do I know of marvels or tests,' said he, 'yet I know of a certain spring not far hence—few escape with their lives from that enchanted place. If you will follow the path, you will come to a place where an ancient chapel stands, small but very beautiful. Next to it grows a tree which is forever green. The spring under that tree bubbles as if it were boiling, yet the water is cold as marble.

" 'Hanging on a chain beside the spring is a basin made of pure gold. And beside the spring is a stone, a great stone unlike any other. If you will fill the basin with water from the spring and pour that water over the stone, you shall see a marvelous sight indeed. A wild wind will rise, and a tempest will break over your head with thunder and lightning and rain and sleet that will drive every beast in the forest to cover. If you can endure that storm, you shall indeed be more fortunate than any other knight who has come this way.'

4

"When he had pointed out the way, I took my leave and rode on until I found the chapel and the tree. Under that most fair tree the spring bubbled up like a crystal fountain. The golden basin hung there, as the giant had said, and next to it stood the marvelous stone, which looked like a great emerald standing on a base of rubies. I took down the basin, filled it from the spring, and poured water over the stone.

"At once such a storm arose that I can hardly describe it. Lightning blinded my eyes from all directions; rain poured down, mixed with hail and snow and sleet; trees crashed to the earth all around me. I could scarcely stand on my feet. But the storm stopped as suddenly as it had started, and then—it was like joy after sorrow! The sun shone, and the birds flocked to the green tree—so many that they covered every bough on the tree, singing so merrily that all the world rang with their happy song.

"I stood in delight till they finished, but as the song died away, I heard another sound, like that of a troop of horsemen thundering toward the spring. From the noise I thought surely it must be many men, yet it was only one knight. A huge, grim warrior on a great, strong horse rode toward me, looking as fierce as a lion. As he came, he called out in challenge, crying, 'Villain, you shall pay dearly for the damage you have caused to these woods!'

"We rushed together in battle, but I was no match for that warrior. My spear broke to splinters on his shield, and soon he struck me so hard that I was knocked off onto the ground. He left me lying there. Without a word he took my horse and rode away. I did not dare to follow him, nor did I know where he had gone. Wounded and alone, without a horse, there was little that I could do.

"At last I arose and took off my armor—I could not choose but leave it there in order to walk the more easily. Thus I made my way home, disgraced, on foot, and defeated."

When Calogrant had finished his tale, he hung his head in shame. "Cousin," cried Ywain. "Why did you not tell me of this before? I would gladly have avenged you on that knight, and I shall do so yet, if I can!"

"Oho," said Sir Kay, "listen to the hero! It is plain to see that you drank your share of the cup today, Ywain. What brave words there are in a bottle of wine! Arm yourself now and ride forth before your courage wanes; go right away, tonight! If you should wait until morning, you might not be quite so eager."

"What words are these, good Kay?" said the queen. "How can you let your tongue run on so? It is your own worst enemy."

"It does not matter, my lady," said Ywain. "I have no wish to

6

quarrel with Kay. Let him speak as he pleases, for he cannot anger me with his words."

As they spoke, King Arthur came out and took his place by the queen. When all the knights had greeted the king, Guinevere told him of Calogrant's strange adventure.

"By my father's soul," Arthur exclaimed, "I swear I must see that marvel with my own eyes!" Then and there he declared that he and whosoever should wish to ride with him would make a journey to the enchanted spring no later than Saint John's Eve. As everyone knows, that is the most magical night of the year, a time when mortal men often meet fairies and elves.

All the knights of the court rejoiced when they heard of the king's plan. There was no page so young that he did not at once set his heart on joining that company. Ywain alone was cast down at the news. He wished nothing more than to go by himself, for he had sworn to avenge his cousin. This, he feared, could not be if he rode with the king's company; King Arthur would let Sir Kay have the combat if he should ask it, or perhaps Sir Gawain, that peerless knight, would claim it before someone else could. Ywain's only chance was to leave by himself before the others were ready.

And so he decided to be on his way at once. He called for his horse and armor, warning his squire that no one must know he had gone. He took no leave of the court, but long before dawn, while everyone else was asleep, he mounted his horse and rode alone into the forest.

He rode through mountains and wilderness and passed through many a valley, until at last he came to the clearing where the giant herdsman kept his wild beasts. The strange, ugly creature showed Ywain the path to the spring, and he followed that trail until he

could see the chapel. It gleamed in the sunlight, and alongside were the tree and the bubbling spring. Quickly he seized the golden basin and poured water over the great green stone. No sooner had he emptied the last drop than there was a roar of wind and thunder, lightning flashed, and a torrent of rain and hail fell from the sky. Then after the storm it grew calm again, and the birds sang in the green tree. He had not long to wait until he saw a huge knight in red riding toward him with the speed of a bird in flight.

Grimly the two knights joined in battle. Each drove his spear into the other's shield, but neither could unhorse the other. When their lances were shattered and useless, they drew swords and dealt each other many a stroke until their shields were cut to pieces and blood ran from their hauberks in streams. They struck so at each other's helmets that sparks flew from their swords. At last Ywain cut through the Red Knight's helm and gave him a mortal wound.

9

The Red Knight knew that he was near death. He turned and fled. Ywain pursued him as fast as he could, for he did not want to lose sight of him. What if he could not prove he had fulfilled his oath? He spurred his horse on, and rode faster and faster on the Red Knight's heels, until suddenly he found they had come to the gate of a castle. A length behind the Red Knight, he followed onto the bridge of the castle. At either end of this bridge was an iron portcullis, but Ywain was riding too fast to take care. As the Red Knight passed into the castle, both portcullis gates dropped very suddenly; Ywain was caught on a narrow bridge between two sets of iron bars.

2: The Ring of Invisibility

YWAIN LEAPT OFF his horse and looked for a way out, but there was none. He was trapped. To jump off the bridge into the dark moat beneath would be foolish indeed; no man in armor could swim in those depths. Yet he was almost ready to do just this when a door opened in the castle wall, just beyond the inner gate, and a maiden came out and spoke to him.

"Sir," she said, "this is no place for you to be found. The knight to whom you have dealt his deathblow is our champion and defender. The men of the castle will soon seek you, and if they find you, they will surely kill you. But you were once kind to me when I was at Arthur's court, and I intend to repay that favor—you see I have recognized you, Sir Ywain. I shall lend you my ring. With the stone turned in, against your palm, no man will be able to see you. Take it, and when this danger is past, you shall return it to me."

Through the bars of the portcullis she slipped the ring on his finger, and just in time. At that moment a great crowd came running out of the main gate of the castle, looking for the attacker. They were sure he must be there, for they could see his horse and there was no sign of a drowning man in the moat. But when they pulled up the portcullis, Ywain, who was now invisible to them, slipped past to the door where the maiden awaited him and went with her into an inner room.

The men of the castle could not believe their eyes, for there was no trace at all of the stranger they were sure had been trapped there. Some said he must have escaped through witchcraft, and others asked if he might have grown wings. One thing they knew: no man could escape from that bridge alive. To make sure, they went through the castle searching for him, high and low. But they looked in vain. When they came into the room where Ywain was, they could not see him because of the ring. Roaring with rage, they swept on through the castle. Ywain breathed a sigh of relief as their cries faded off in the distance.

"Now," said the maiden, "you shall be safe if you will stay quietly here in this room and not show your head until I can get you away. The gates of the castle are locked. You must stay here until they give up the search. If anyone should find you, your life would certainly be forfeit. I am the handmaid of the lady of the castle; I am called Lunette. Now I will bring you food and drink."

When Lunette had left, Ywain looked about the room. It was richly and comfortably furnished. There was a small window in the wall, and through it came the sound of a funeral procession. Ywain was sad at the thought that now he would never get any token of vic-

tory from the Red Knight. Kay and the other knights of the court would not believe his story when he could give them no proof. With a sigh he went over and peered through the narrow window to see the procession wind by. There among the mourners he saw a lady as white as milk. So lovely was she, despite her grief, that Ywain thought he had never seen anyone half so beautiful. As he gazed at her, he quite forgot Sir Kay and Sir Calogrant and the Red Knight.

Lunette soon returned with a roasted capon, bread, and a jug of wine. She spread a white linen cloth and invited Ywain to eat. But Ywain, although he had eaten nothing all that day, could not turn his eyes from that lovely lady. He asked Lunette who she might be.

"That is my lady, Laudine, the mistress of this castle and your most bitter enemy," said Lunette. "But you must come from the window now, Sir Ywain. Someone might notice you standing there, for I see you are not using my ring."

Ywain stepped back, but he could not help glancing once more over his shoulder. He could think of nothing but the beauty of the lady Laudine. Now he was doubly a prisoner: he could not stir from this room lest the men of the castle should set upon him, and he had no wish to leave if he could, for then he might never come near his beautiful enemy.

Lunette saw that Ywain had little appetite for his meal, and asked him whether it was not to his taste. "Fair friend," said Ywain, "the meal is excellent. However, the lady I saw through the window is even more to my mind. If only I could win her! Then I should be the most fortunate of men." He sighed. "What a cruel chance that she whom I would love and honor above all ladies should consider me her enemy."

14

Lunette looked thoughtful. "Perhaps," she said, "she will not always think of you in this way. It may be that I can help you. In any case, I shall try my best. Somehow I will find a way both to release you from danger and to gain you the prize you seek. For now, though, you must stay safely hidden. Take care that my ring is turned the right way on your finger until I return, lest anyone enter the room."

Leaving him, she went to her mistress, who held her in the highest favor. "My lady Laudine," she said, "you must know that King Arthur and all his knights are on their way to your spring. Who will defend your land now? If these knights are allowed to raise storm after storm, your fields and forests will be destroyed."

Laudine knew this very well. "But what can I do?" she asked. "The Red Knight, who was my only champion, lies dead, alas! No man now living is brave enough to defend me against the king and his knights, for they are the best in the world."

"Say not so," said Lunette, "for it is clear that one man lives who is still better a knight than the one you have lost."

"Better than my Red Knight!" said Laudine. "There could be none better than he. What can you mean, Lunette?"

"Tell me, my lady," said Lunette, "when two knights fight in fair combat, which is the better man?"

"Why, he who wins the battle," answered Laudine.

"Then," said Lunette, "the knight who conquered the Red Knight is surely a better man. This is the man you need to defend your spring."

Laudine gasped in anger, but try as she might she could find no other answer. After a while she said, "But who is this man? May he be willing to be my champion?"

16

"Lady, he is one of the finest knights alive," the maiden answered. "I know that he is Sir Ywain, son of King Urien, and as noble a knight as you can find anywhere. And I know, too, that he loves you dearly and would willingly serve you for the rest of his life."

In the end Laudine agreed to forgive Ywain and to receive him with favor. Perhaps she might even give him her hand in marriage if he should prove so worthy a knight. "But can you send for him in time?" she asked. "King Arthur is already on his way, and may arrive at my spring tomorrow. Can you find Sir Ywain and bring him here so soon?"

Lunette smiled. "Lady, he shall be with you tomorrow. It would be well for you to call a meeting of your council so that you may have their advice on whether you should accept this noble knight as your champion. I think they will be glad of the offer. For my part I promise that he will come before the day is half spent."

Laudine did just as Lunette advised. She sent word to all her councillors to meet with her in the morning. Meanwhile Lunette returned to the anxious prisoner and merrily told him of her success.

When morning came, Lunette had rich robes of scarlet and gold ready for Ywain to wear. "Now, sir," she said, "you must give back my ring, for you shall have no further need of it. Be of good cheer, my noble lord, for your captivity soon will be over."

Gaily she led him by the hand into Laudine's chamber. There stood Laudine, as lovely a lady as ever lived. She waited for Ywain to greet her. But Sir Ywain hung back. He could not find a word to say. Lunette was more merry than ever, laughing at his confusion. She said, "Come, sir knight, you need not be afraid—my lady will not bite you! Where is your courage, Sir Ywain?"

Ywain dropped on his knee and said, "Lady, I beg your forgiveness if I have offended against you. Never would I hurt you willingly, for truly my heart is yours since my first sight of you. Do what you will with me, for I am willing to live or die for your sake."

She asked, "Will you dare promise to defend my land for me even against Arthur and all his knights?"

"I will defend you," answered Ywain, "against any man alive."

Pleased with his answer, the lady gave him her hand. He rose and followed her to the great hall where all her councillors were gathered. "Sirs," she said, "this noble knight offers to defend my spring. How say you? Shall I accept him as my champion?"

The knights of her land looked at Ywain and saw a fine-looking young man, strong, noble, and handsome. Among themselves they murmured that he looked worthy to be an emperor. The steward of the castle answered for them all, "My lady Laudine, we know well that King Arthur is on his way and that he will try to win this land if he can. We have need of a stalwart champion. But tell us this. What does this knight ask as his reward if he is willing to defend us against such a terrible challenge?"

"He asks my hand in marriage," answered Laudine. "He is the son of a king, and I believe him to be wise, brave, and courteous."

It did not take long for them to agree that if Ywain could defend the spring and prove himself worthy of their lady's love, he might then claim her as his wife. There was no time now for further talk, for word came that Arthur had passed their borders and was fast approaching the spring. Ywain must prepare for the battle.

3: The Ring of Safety

As ARTHUR RODE up to the spring with a great troop of knights, Sir Kay said, "Where is the boaster who said he would avenge his cousin here? For all his brave words before the queen, I see him not when battle is near! He would not dare even to look at the knight he bragged he would conquer."

"Peace, Sir Kay," said Gawain quickly. "I think we shall hear of Sir Ywain today unless he is dead or imprisoned."

"We shall see," said Kay, with a scornful laugh.

The king drew water from the spring and sprinkled it on the stone. At once the storm arose as terrible as before. The king and his men thought that they would be killed by the violent gales and sharp, icy sleet.

Ywain, hearing the roar of the thunder, mounted at once and rode toward the spring, as swift as the wind of the storm. As soon as they could see him coming, Kay begged the king to let him take the battle. The king granted his boon.

Ywain drew near, and Kay jumped on his horse. Then Ywain rejoiced when he saw it was Kay who rode against him—but Kay could not know who was his opponent. Ywain had good hopes that he could avenge the rude words Kay had spoken against him and joined battle with all his might. Soon he knocked Kay from his saddle so that the knight with the mocking tongue fell on the earth with such a crash that his helmet drove into the ground.

Ywain had no wish to do him further harm. He alighted, took Sir Kay's horse, and led it to King Arthur. "Sir king," he said, "I give you this steed, for you may have use for it."

Arthur asked, "But what man are you?"

Ywain pulled off his helmet and knelt before his king. "Lord," said he, "it is I, Ywain."

Now the king and his knights were happy indeed, except for Sir Kay who had said that Ywain would not dare to come. It was a bad time for Kay as he lay forgotten on the ground. Few had been sorry to see him take a fall; none had so much as a glance for him now as they crowded around Sir Ywain, and Gawain especially cried out with joy to find his dear friend well.

The king then asked Ywain to tell them how he came to be there, and Ywain told him all that had happened since he had left the court, adding, "My lady Laudine asks that you, Sire, and all your knights honor her by coming with me to the castle, where you will be most welcome guests." The king agreed readily, and Ywain sent a message to Laudine at once, bidding her to prepare to receive her noble guests. This good news made the lady exceedingly glad.

Quickly Laudine bade her men prepare a royal welcome for the king. The men of the castle rode forth, dressed in their richest robes and mounted on the finest of steeds, to meet the king and his company. They rode along streets lined with gay banners to the sound of trumpets and pipes. The maidens of the town danced before the king, and the lady Laudine herself, regally dressed in purple and ermine, greeted him with gracious words of welcome.

For eight days and nights they held a great feast in the castle. Days were spent hunting in the woods and forest, evenings in feasting with singing and dancing and much merriment. But then the time came for the king to depart, and Gawain did all he could to persuade his friend Ywain to come with the court.

"If you stay here with your lady," he said, "how can you perform deeds of arms and prove yourself worthy to wed her? A knight must win fame for his chivalry, then his lady will love him the better. Come with me, Ywain. We two shall bear away the prize at many a tournament!"

Ywain had no wish to leave his lovely Laudine, but Gawain argued long. Kay, who still smarted from his defeat, overheard the two knights. "Sir Gawain," said Kay, "you might as well save your breath. Our fierce warrior here has found that one battle was quite enough. He does not care to risk his neck again when it would be so much more pleasant to lie back all day on pillows and soft couches, taking his ease among the fair ladies."

"Kay!" said Sir Gawain. "That is enough. Sir Ywain would not say such words of malice against any man, I am sure."

But Kay's words stung Ywain. He went to his lady and asked her permission to take his leave for a while so that he might win fame and honor for her sake. "Sir," said Laudine, "I give you leave for a certain term. But if you love me indeed, you must return in a year and a day. Today is the eve of Saint John. If you do not return by Saint John's Day next year, I swear you shall lose my love forever."

"Lady," replied the knight, "I shall not fail to keep that day, if it be in my power. But, madame, you must know well that when a knight roams through the world, he may meet with many mis-

fortunes. He may fall ill or be taken prisoner. Therefore, I pray you that if I should against my will be prevented from coming on the day you appoint, you will not hold it against me."

Laudine granted this. "However," she said, "I give you this ring to keep you from just such misfortune." Slipping a ring with a gleaming blue stone onto Ywain's finger, she told him, "As long as you are true to all you have promised, this ring will keep you safe from harm. You shall never fall sick or be wounded in battle, nor can any prison hold you. But if you should break your faith to me, the stone will lose its virtue. Pray God that may never happen! Keep the ring well, Sir Ywain, for my sake. Do not forget to think of Laudine."

Sir Ywain thanked his dear lady many times over. He thought that a year away from her was almost more than he could bear. At last he took his leave of her.

Now Gawain was glad, and the men mounted their steeds and prepared to ride off. They did not forget to bid farewell to the lovely lady of the spring and her charming handmaid, Lunette. Gawain, the courteous, especially thanked Lunette for her help to his friend, saying that he would come at her call if ever she should have need of him.

Ywain and Gawain went on their way to many a joust and tournament. No other knights were a match for those two. They both won prizes far and wide, and their fame spread throughout the land. For a full twelve months they rode in every tournament, and Ywain won great renown everywhere he went. Thus the year passed, month after month, until Saint John's Day had come and gone. Only then did Ywain recall his promise to the lady Laudine.

26

He was at Arthur's court at that season. Ywain had not thought
of his lady for many a day. Now when he looked at the ring she had
given him, he saw to his horror that the color of the stone had
changed. What had been a bright and shining blue was now a dull,
muddy green. He knew that this meant he had been false to his
word.

In deep shame and confusion, Ywain hastily rose from his seat
to leave the company of King Arthur's knights. But as he did so, he
saw a maiden muffled in a black cloak and riding on a black palfrey coming swiftly toward the pavilion where they were gathered
around the king. She reined in her horse before the tent, but did
not alight. Still mounted on her steed, she looked at the king and
his knights, letting her cloak fall back from her face.

It was the damsel Lunette. "Hail, my lord king," she said. "My lady Laudine sends greetings to you, Sire, and to good Sir Gawain and all the true knights of your court—but not to the false Sir Ywain. To him she sends word that she forbids him ever to come into her presence again, for he has broken his solemn promise and betrayed her shamefully." Now she looked directly at Ywain, saying, "False traitor, from this day on you shall be despised by all honorable men, nor shall you ever win the wife you once desired so much. My lady bids you send back her ring. It is not fitting for such as you to defile the gift of Laudine."

She pulled the ring from his hand, turned her horse, and rode off again.

Sir Ywain stood as still as a stone. His shame and sorrow so weighed upon him that he could not speak or move. Nor could any of the others there find words to say to him until at last with a cry of despair he turned and ran off from the company, and went alone into the forest before anyone could follow him.

And so Sir Ywain disappeared. No one knew what had become of him. For many days they searched for him, but it was in vain. He was nowhere to be found.

4: The Lion and the Dragon

DEEP IN THE forest, Ywain wandered alone for many nights and days. Grief for his double loss—the loss of his honor as a chivalrous knight and the loss of the lady Laudine—nearly drove him out of his wits. He lived as best he could on roots and berries and herbs, growing thinner and weaker by the day, until one day he came upon a small hut where a hermit lived. By now Ywain's beard and hair were long and matted, his clothing crumpled and filthy. The hermit took one alarmed look and fled back into his hut, barring his door behind him.

But the hermit was a holy and charitable man. He had pity on all God's creatures, and would not willingly see any suffer, so he placed barley bread and water outside his window where Ywain might find it. Ywain ate this humble fare with a far better appetite

29

than ever he had felt at the king's high table, for when a man is half
starved the driest crust of bread will taste like a feast fit for a prince.
Refreshed and strengthened, he blessed the good hermit, and went
to find a stream where he might wash. There he rested a while and
fell into a deep sleep.

Now, as he slept under a tree, three ladies came riding by that
way. One who rode on a white palfrey was a lady of noble birth who
had often been at Arthur's court. She recognized Sir Ywain at once,
despite his sadly changed appearance. Turning to her handmaids,
she bade them ride quickly to the manor house, which was not far
off, and bring fresh clothing, arms, and a horse fit for this noble
knight. "Make haste," she said; "while you are gone I shall stay
with him and see whether perchance I can be of help. For I have
here a precious ointment, the gift of Morgan le Fay; its magic
powers may help to heal his body and mind."

While her maidens did as she bade them, she knelt by Ywain's
side and gently anointed his face and hands with the magic ointment. Ywain awoke with a new strength and a calmer mind, and
gazed in wonder at the lady by his side. He was about to rise, to pay
her due honor, but she held out a hand to stop him. "Nay, fair sir,"
she said, "rest a while yet. You shall feel the better for it. Soon my
maidens shall return with clothing, arms, and a horse. That will be
time enough for you to rise refreshed from your rest."

"Fair lady," said Ywain, "I know not how, yet I feel strengthened
already, though it has been many a week since I had a taste of meat
or wine. I think I must owe to you the new vigor I feel."

"Good Sir Ywain," said the lady, "you feel the virtue of a precious salve I have used to bring you back to yourself."

30

"Lady, I thank you with all my heart," said the knight, "and I would be a poor wretch indeed if I did not promise to give you such help as I can, should you ever have need of a knight. Tell me, if you will, who you are, and how I may be of service to you."

"I am the younger daughter," she said, "of the Lord of Noirespine, a great lord in this land. I thank you for your offer and will remember it if ever I need your help. But now, good sir, it is enough that I see you well again."

Soon the two maidens returned with all that was needful for Ywain, who thanked the ladies many times over before they took their leave. The daughter of the Lord of Noirespine wished him to come to her father's manor to stay there as their guest, but Ywain courteously refused.

At last she had to accept his answer and leave him there in the wood. Sir Ywain felt far better now than he had for many a day, but still his heart was sore as he thought of the lady Laudine and the deep disgrace he had brought on himself.

Now as Ywain rode on through the depths of the forest, suddenly he heard a hideous cry. He turned in the direction from which the noise seemed to come and found there a most strange sight. A dragon had captured a wild lion by the tail. As the lion struggled to escape, the dragon breathed flames that scorched the lion terribly, making it quite impossible for him to turn and fight back.

Quickly Ywain determined to come to the aid of the lion, for the poisonous, fiery dragon was clearly the more dangerous beast of the two. With his shield before his face, to keep off the flames which spurted from its nostrils and mouth, he rushed at the dragon with his sword and slashed through the wicked creature's neck. But the head still hung clamped on the lion's tail, and Ywain saw no other way to rid the lion of the dragon's jaws than to cut off the tip of the lion's tail. This he therefore did, though he thought that now he would surely have to fight the lion as well.

But, to Ywain's surprise, the lion dropped to the ground and fawned like a dog at the knight's feet. He sat on his haunches and lifted a paw in homage and thanks to the knight, then crouched down again and licked Ywain's feet. Sir Ywain, touched at the beast's gratitude, patted and stroked him and spoke to him kindly. At this the beast jumped up for joy and bounded in circles for all the world as if he had been a tame puppy.

When Ywain had cleaned the dragon's poisonous blood from his sword, he thought it time to ride on his way. The lion followed along at his side, never once leaving him, until a time came when man and beast both began to feel pangs of hunger. Now the lion sniffed the wind, pawed at the ground, and growled a bit. Ywain understood and nodded his encouragement. Off bounded the lion into the wood, where he quickly found some game. When he had caught it—a fine, fat hare—and killed it with a bite in the throat, he picked it up and brought it back and laid it at Ywain's feet. It was now nearly nighttime, and Ywain thought he would ride no further. He made a fire of moss and boughs, and cooked the meat on a spit of green wood. Thus Ywain and the lion dined well enough, though the knight missed salt and wine with his meal.

And so, for a fortnight and more, the knight and the lion kept company, and the lion found meat to feed them both. Their drink was water from forest streams, and Ywain's good horse fed on leaves and grass. At length it befell that by pure chance they

wandered into a place that Ywain knew at once. There, under the fairest green tree in the world, bubbled the spring he remembered so well, and close beside it stood the small chapel.

Ywain looked deep into the clear water of the spring. He felt his old grief return in all its pain. Covering his eyes with his arm, he dropped to the ground and lay there so still that he might well have been dead. As he did so, his sword slipped from its scabbard, grazing the side of Sir Ywain's neck. When the lion saw a trickle of blood and the knight lying motionless on the ground, he thought that Ywain was certainly dead, and fell into terrible grief. Moaning dismally to himself, he pulled Ywain's sword aside and, with his paws, pushed the hilt under a stone so that the point of the blade stood up.

The lion was just about to jump on the sword and kill himself for pure sorrow when Ywain stirred and sighed and rose again to his feet. Now the lion was overjoyed to see his master unhurt. He licked Ywain's face and feet and bounded about lightheartedly. Ywain smiled at the lion's antics, but his heart was still heavy with sorrow. He sighed as he looked at the lovely scene and mournfully complained aloud.

In the chapel a damsel sat, alone and closely imprisoned. Through a chink in the chapel wall she could hear Ywain's voice. She called out, "What is that I hear?"

"A man," he answered, "passing by. But who are you behind that wall?"

"I am the most wretched creature alive," said the maiden in the chapel.

"Ah, no," said Sir Ywain. "Whatever your sorrow may be, it is joy

34

compared to mine. For once I was a noble knight whose name was honored throughout the land. I had wealth and men at my command, and all this have I lost through my own folly. But most of all I live in woe because I have lost the love of the most beautiful lady alive."

"Is that all?" said the maiden's voice. "You have your life and your freedom. Be glad of that, sir, and pity the sorry wretch that speaks to you. For I was the chief and highest in favor of the hand-maids of a great lady nearby. Now men falsely call me a traitor, though I meant only to bring her happiness! They have thrown me into prison here. There is no knight who will come to my aid, and therefore I shall be burnt alive tomorrow without fail."

Asked Ywain, "What if a knight should come to defend you?"

"Alas, sir," said the unhappy maid, "I know of only two knights who would rescue me if they knew of my plight. One is Sir Gawain, the goodly knight, but I could not find him at the court, and I fear he is far away. As for the other—there is no man who knows where Sir Ywain has gone."

"Ywain is here," the knight replied, "and he shall not let you die alone. I am he, and you are Lunette—now I know your voice. Can it be that my lady blames you for my shameful treatment of her?"

"Do not blame my lady Laudine," Lunette answered at once. "The steward and his two brothers were ever jealous of me because I always had my lady's ear and she loved me especially. They falsely accused me of helping you to kill the Red Knight, her former cham-pion, leaving her defenseless against all enemies. At first my lady would hear none of it, but in the end they so aroused the people against me that she had no choice but to agree that a trial by combat should settle my guilt. But the steward would only grant me a week

36

in which to find a defender, and in those few days I could find no
trace of either you or Sir Gawain. And so you find me here con-
demned. I must die in the flames tomorrow."

"Not while I have life in my body," Sir Ywain declared. "I shall
be there to defend you."

"That may not be so easy," she said, "for the false steward has
sworn that any man who rides in my cause must face both him and
his two brothers at once."

"By the grace of God," said Ywain, "I may yet be able to avenge
you on all three of those foul traitors."

Now Ywain departed from her, with his lion by his side, to seek
a resting place for the night. He would have need of all his strength
on the morrow, if he must face three armed men at a time.

5: The Giant Harpin

BEFORE LONG SIR Ywain **same** to a splendid manor house surrounded by a high wall. The porters opened to his call, but when they saw the lion, they fled in terror, crying out, "Do not let that beast through our gates. He will murder us all!"

"Do not be afraid," said Ywain. "This lion is my dear comrade. He will not harm anyone who does not harm me. Give us both shelter, I pray you, for if he remains outside, then I must, too."

Fearfully they let him pass, and all the folk within wondered greatly when they saw a knight ride in with a lion at his heels, trotting along as quietly as any tame dog. They made him welcome and greeted him graciously, but Ywain could not help but see that something was very much wrong. It could not be just fear of his lion that made every soul in the manor look bowed down with grief. For

38

all their courteous words to him, he could see the tears on their cheeks and hear the sadness in their voices. Ywain observed them all carefully as he sat down with the household for the evening meal.

At last he felt he must ask his host what might be the cause of their sorrow. "Indeed, sir," answered the old lord of that manor, "we mourn for the disaster that is sure to befall us tomorrow. There is a giant who lives nearby, an evil monster called Harpin of the Mountain. He is the cause of our suffering. He has robbed and laid waste my lands until I have nothing left but this manor. Worse still, he has killed two of my sons and now holds the other four prisoners. He swears he will kill all four tomorrow under my very eyes, as he did their two brothers. He hates us all, because I would not give him my only daughter in marriage. Now, he says, he hates her, too, and will not take her for his wife. He demands that I let him have her so that he may give her to the dirtiest low scoundrel in his household. Alas, that I could get no word of this to Sir Gawain! He would have come to our aid, for my wife is his sister. Never would Gawain allow that giant to slaughter his nephews and carry off his niece to such disgrace!"

"Fair sir," said Ywain, "for Gawain's sake, I will fight this giant, if he arrives in good time. But I have made a vow to another, which I must fulfill at noon tomorrow, and I cannot tarry here if he is late."

The lord jumped up and praised God for this offer of help. The people of his household joined in blessing the knight who had brought them hope. Just then the lady of the manor came into the room, leading her daughter by the hand. The young girl was as lovely as she could be, for all that her bright beauty was dimmed by fear and sorrow. When mother and daughter heard that Ywain

would come to their help, both dropped to their knees and thanked
him humbly. Ywain would not allow Gawain's sister and niece to
kneel before him. He lifted them up, saying, "I pray that God will
help me defeat your enemy, and that he may come in time in the
morning, for I must be on my way long before noon."

The ladies of the household showed Ywain to the chamber where
he was to spend the night, but they were much afraid of the lion. No
one dared come into the chamber while the lion was there, and they
all barred their doors when they went to their beds for fear that the
lion might come out in the night.

When the sun arose, Ywain armed himself and waited until the
morning was nearly half gone. Then he went to the lord and said,

40

"I am grieved that I cannot wait for your terrible foe, but I do not dare to wait any longer. I have promised another my help this noon, and I should rather die than fail to be there."

"For the love of Sir Gawain," pleaded the lord, "wait with us a little longer. I will give you half my land if you will only help us in this terrible need. Indeed, you may have my daughter to wife, and she is as lovely and noble as any lady in the land."

"Gladly would I be of service to you," Sir Ywain replied, "and I would not wish any reward at all, but I must not break my word to the one who awaits me."

The poor maiden broke into tears, beseeching him to stay, and everyone there added pitiful pleas. Ywain was torn between desire to help them and fears for Lunette, who would surely be burnt for his sake if he did not arrive by noon. He would have had to go on his way, but at that moment a messenger came with the news that the giant Harpin had arrived.

He appeared now in the field in front of the manor, driving the lord's four sons before him. The wretched young men were bound hand and foot and clad in rags. As they stumbled forward, the terrible giant lashed them with a huge iron rod, so that blood ran all over their half-naked backs.

Stopping before the gate, the giant cried out, "Here are your sons, but they'll not live long unless you give me your daughter at once. I shall give her to the worst ruffian I know to make her suffer for her pride! Come, give me the jade or look the last on your sons!"

In answer they opened the gates, and out rode Ywain armed for combat. When the giant saw him, he said, "Oho, sir knight, whoever sent you here cannot have loved you! You may see how I have dealt with four strong young knights. Do you want me to treat you in the same way?"

"Do your worst," said Ywain, and charged against him. The giant, who fought with no protection but a coat made from the hide of a bull, was soon wounded by the point of Ywain's spear. But this did not stop him from dealing many savage blows with his great iron bar until Ywain reeled and fell on his horse's neck. Now the lion had followed his master out, and when he saw him hurt, he charged at the giant with a ferocious roar. In no time at all he had torn the flesh from the giant's back.

The giant turned with a howl and struck at the lion, but the lion was much too quick for him. By now Sir Ywain had recovered himself, and with one good stroke of his sword he pierced to the giant's heart. Harpin of the Mountain fell like a tree crashing in the forest.

The men of the manor opened the gates wide, and many a joyful man and woman ran out to look at the dead giant. The four brothers were quickly released and welcomed by their whole family. Their sister was not the last to embrace Sir Ywain with tears of pure joy. But Ywain was anxious to be on his way and would not linger to receive their thanks. With his lion beside him, he rode quickly off toward the chapel by the spring.

Ywain now had to ride like the wind, for it was almost noon, and he greatly feared he might be too late to save Lunette's life. As at last he came to the appointed place, he found a great fire already kindled. The maiden Lunette was bound with cords, ready to be thrown into the flames. He had arrived not a minute too soon. Indeed, he thought, God and truth are on my side, and my lion shall lend me aid. We four should be a match against any three!

42

Spurring his horse into the midst of the crowd, he cried, "Stop, I bid you, false traitors! You shall not harm this innocent maid while I live to defend her."

Men moved aside for him quickly enough when they saw the lion at his heels. He rode straight to the place where Lunette knelt, surrounded by grieving ladies of the court who wept for her. Ywain reached out and gently raised Lunette to her feet, saying, "Whoever accuses this damsel of any wrong must prove his case by fighting me, for I stake my life on her truth."

"Then order that lion out of the way," said the false steward, "for you shall have to fight all three of us by yourself."

"I can do without his help," said Ywain, "for the truth is on my side." He ordered his lion to go back to the edge of the field. There the lion lay down and watched, his tail on the ground.

6: The Knight of the Lion

THE STEWARD AND his two brothers bore down at once on Ywain, who defended himself so well that all three broke their lances on his shield. Indeed one of his strokes was worth three of theirs, and soon he swept the steward from his horse. It did not, however, take the steward long to rise from the ground, draw his sword, and rush back into the fight. Now the three fought Ywain from three different sides, so that it became harder and harder for him to fend off their blows.

But when the lion saw that his master was hard pressed, he would not stay at the side any longer but rushed to Ywain's

45

defense. With a bound he leapt on the steward's back, tearing him to pieces. With the steward dead, the battle was even again. Ywain could not make the lion leave the field, although he tried to send him off. Whatever he might say, the lion was determined to fight by his side.

For their part the false steward's brothers lost no time in attacking the lion, and gave him some terrible wounds. Not even that could stop the faithful beast. The lion brought them down, both horse and rider. The brothers soon saw that they had no choice but to yield to Ywain. Now a glad cry went up from the crowd, for Lunette was much loved. Ywain led the maiden by the hand to her mistress Laudine, who received her tenderly.

"Sir knight," said Laudine, "I thank you from the bottom of my heart. But for you and your lion, this sweet lady would have been destroyed through the malice of those three false brothers. Now come and let us tend to your wounds."

Ywain cared nothing for his own wounds, but he grieved for his faithful lion who was sorely hurt. Still he would not reveal himself to Laudine. "I thank you, lady," he said, "but no, I cannot stay here."

"Yet for your lion's sake," urged Laudine, "I beg you to stay and rest with us, for the poor beast is much injured. We shall try our best to honor you and wish you to share in our joy."

"Nay, madame," said Ywain, "that cannot be. I shall never know joy until I have regained the good will of my lady."

Laudine could not know that she was the lady with whom his hope of joy rested. She pressed him to stay. When she saw that he would not, she said, "Then, sir, if you must go, at least tell us your name that we may know whom to thank."

46

"Lady," said Ywain, "you may call me the Knight of the Lion."

"Then farewell, Knight of the Lion," said the lady Laudine. "May God soon grant you happiness."

Before he left that place, however, Ywain had a private word with Lunette, the only one who knew who her rescuer really was. She promised him she would do all she could to persuade Laudine to receive him back into her favor. Then he bade her farewell and rode on in search of a place where he and his lion might rest and recover from their wounds. By now the lion was so weak that Ywain had to carry him on his shield. Soon enough he came to another castle, where the good lord and his people took them in and cared for both knight and beast until they were well again.

During the time that had passed since Ywain rescued the lion, it happened that the Lord of Noirespine fell sick and died. He left his lands and wealth to his two daughters, for he had no other heir. The elder of the two sisters was a proud, ungenerous woman, and she made up her mind she would take all the inheritance for herself. Her father was hardly in his grave before she rode in haste to Arthur's court to demand a trial by combat to prove her rights against her younger sister. Then she went in search of Sir Gawain and begged his aid as her champion.

Gawain did not wish to refuse a lady who asked for his help. Though he was troubled, being not at all sure her cause was right, he finally consented to fight on her behalf. He added, however, "This must be a secret between you and me. If you tell anyone who your knight is, you will lose my help."

The lady agreed willingly enough and rode home in triumph, sure that no one could defeat Gawain in combat. The younger

48

sister, hearing the news that a combat had been appointed, must now find a knight to defend her cause.

But when the younger sister rode to court and, of course, asked for Gawain's aid, he had to tell her he could not help her, though he did not tell her why. She thought then of Sir Ywain. It had not been very long ago that he had promised her he would come to her aid if ever she needed him. But how was she to find Ywain when no one knew what had become of him? She was nearly in despair. But while she was at the court, news came from Gawain's sister of the strange Knight of the Lion who had killed a giant and rescued Gawain's nephews and niece. Surely, thought the poor lady, a knight who can conquer a giant would be a strong champion to have on my side. If only I can gain his help!

And so the younger sister went in search of the Knight of the Lion. By herself without any attendant, she rode all over the land, seeking news of that knight. Finally she came to Laudine's castle where she heard how the Knight of the Lion had saved Lunette in battle against three men. But no one there knew where he had gone.

She had almost given up her search when she came to the castle where Ywain and his lion had been cared for after the battle. The people of the castle told her that he could not be far away since he had left only that morning. With new hope the lady rode on as fast as her horse would go until at last she saw Sir Ywain riding along with the lion trotting by his side.

Ywain halted and stared in surprise. There before his eyes was the lady who had cared for him when he was weak and ill in the forest. And she, of course, was overjoyed to find that the Knight of the Lion was Ywain.

When she had told him of her trouble, Ywain agreed at once to defend her. "But you must promise," he said to her, "not to tell anyone who I am. I will fight for you as the Knight of the Lion."

Now they set forth for Arthur's court, where the combat was to be held. It was a very long way, too far to travel in one day. At night they must rest somewhere. As the sun went down, they came close to a castle, and were glad of a chance for shelter.

But as they drew close, people came out to meet them, crying, "Turn back, rash knight! Do not enter the Castle of Misadventure!" They caught at his reins, calling out that he would regret his folly if he dared to come into their castle.

Ywain thought this a discourteous welcome, but he rode on to the gate. There the porter glared at the travelers, saying, "Enter in evil hour! He who comes here learns what ill luck is."

Yet Ywain went on into the courtyard. There he saw an enclosure fenced in with sharp, pointed sticks. Within it sat a great many maidens—perhaps a hundred in all—with their heads bent over their work. They were sewing with silk and golden thread, but their own clothes were of a far different kind. All wore ragged and threadbare smocks, and they wept as they worked. Their thin, hollow faces were pitiful to see.

Ywain and the lady looked in astonishment at this sight. "Gentle maidens," said Ywain, "God be with you. Tell me what sorrow afflicts you, and perhaps I can remedy it."

"Alas, fair sir," answered one of the maidens, "I fear there is no remedy for our sad case. We are prisoners here, as you may see. Some years ago the king of our land came to this castle and asked for shelter. That was the beginning of our woe. For in this castle are two monstrous brothers, said to be the twin sons of a devil. No man may spend a night in the castle without being forced to fight them both; and no man who fights them escapes with his life.

"Our king was a young lad, only fourteen, when he fell into their hands. He could not defend himself against them. Rather than be killed on the spot, he agreed to send them the ransom they asked. We are that ransom. Every year our king must send twelve of the fairest and noblest maidens in the land, for as long as the two monsters live. We poor maidens must spend our lives here, laboring for our cruel masters, unless they should be killed or taken in battle.

"Each of us is forced to do work that is worth a fortune, but we are rewarded with nothing but crusts and water for working from dawn to dusk. Many a man has come to fight the two monsters for our sake, but none has ever returned alive."

"I will deliver you if I can," said Ywain.

With his companions he rode on into the castle itself and demanded shelter for the night. All was provided that they could ask, and no one said a word about the maidens in the courtyard or the evil champions of the place. But in the morning when Ywain arose, the steward of the castle came to his door.

"Sir knight," he said, "it is the custom of this castle that you must fight before you can leave. You must arm yourself to fight two mighty champions. If you should win, you shall be lord of this land."

"I do not want any part of this land," said Ywain, "but I will fight the two champions. If I win, I ask only freedom for the maidens who labor outside."

The steward bowed and led Ywain to the hall where the two monstrous champions, each armed with a club and a mace, waited for him. Ywain thought, These may indeed be sons of a devil, for I never saw human beings so ugly! When the lion saw the evil creatures, he beat his tail on the ground and growled. At once the two monsters demanded that the lion be put out of the place.

54

"The lion must stay with me," said Ywain, "but I will tie him up so that he cannot attack you." His opponents insisted the lion must be tied in another room. At last Ywain led his lion out to the next room, where he tied him firmly to a post.

With the lion safely out of the way, the devilish brothers closed in and battered Ywain hideously until his shield was shattered. Try as he might, Ywain could not seem to repay their blows, for their shields were as strong as they were and the two of them were too much for any man.

In the outer room the lion heard the noise of the battle and grew frenzied and wild to join the fight. Raging, he tore apart the ropes that bound him and rushed to the door, but Ywain had bolted it behind him. The lion dug and scratched at the wood with his claws until at last he had made a hole barely large enough for him to squeeze through. By now Ywain was hard pressed; the daughter of the Lord of Noirespine wept for fear as she saw him beginning to reel under the wicked blows of mace and club. The lion broke out just in time and bore down one of the monsters with a terrible roar.

Ywain's companion could now rejoice, for she could see that the first monster would not rise again. Then Ywain and the lion together made short work of the other, and the combat was over.

The folk of the castle gathered around, begging Ywain to be their lord. It seemed there was no one who was not glad to see the end of those evil masters. But Ywain told them he must not linger, for he had business at court. As soon as he had seen the captive damsels released, he and the lady rode on again with the lion by their side.

7: Ywain and Gawain

ON THE DAY appointed for the trial by combat, the elder sister was ready at Arthur's court. She had no fear of the outcome, for she was confident that no one could possibly stand against Sir Gawain. Gawain himself stayed in a pavilion on the edge of the field where the battle was to be held. He would not fight under his own coat of arms, and he did not want anyone to know who he was.

As midmorning drew on, the elder sister stood before King Arthur, saying, "Sire, here I am as I promised, and my knight stands ready to defend me. My sister has not returned. I do not think she could find anyone who would fight to deprive me of my rights. Therefore, sir king, give me your judgment and let us go."

56

But the king replied, "Be patient a while, for she may yet come."

Just then they saw a knight and a lady riding together toward them. On the knight's shield was the figure of a lion. No one there had seen that shield before so they knew not who he might be. The lady, however, was known to all; it was the younger sister, coming with a knight to defend her rights. "Hail, King Arthur," she said. "This knight is ready to venture his life in my cause."

Now great excitement spread throughout the court, for two unknown knights were about to fight on behalf of the two sisters. Some guessed that the younger sister's champion might be that Knight of the Lion of whose brave deeds they had heard, since he bore on his shield the device of a lion. Others said no, that could not be, since the Knight of the Lion always had a real lion by his side. The lion was not there that day; Sir Ywain had left his quarters very quietly that morning while the lion, exhausted by the fight with the monsters and his struggle to escape from the chamber, was still asleep. Ywain did not need or want his help. This battle was to be a fair combat between two knights—but the lion might not have understood.

Here was a strange combat indeed: neither knight knew that the other was his dearest friend. If either had seen the other's face, he would never have consented to fight. But since they did not know, they took each other for bitter enemies, for the sake of the sisters they had sworn to defend. So although the two men in truth loved each other dearly, at this moment each intended harm to the other, and they rode at each other fiercely.

The king and his court watched the battle closely, and were astonished at the skill of both knights. Never had they seen a more

closely matched pair. Grimly the battle went on; when both spears were broken, the two knights exchanged sword strokes, blow for blow, and each defended himself equally well. They fought for hour after hour, and neither had the advantage of the other.

When both were bleeding and weary, when their shields were shattered to pieces and their helmets split, they agreed to halt and rest a while. But it was not long before they were brought fresh shields and arms, and clashed together again.

The king began to feel alarmed. It seemed that neither of these good knights was a better man than the other, and he saw no way of stopping the fight before they both lost their lives. That would indeed be a pity, he thought, for never had he seen such champions. The queen and the other knights all tried to persuade the two sisters to halt the fight and let the king decide the quarrel, but the elder sister would not agree. She said she would never tell her knight to stop until she had won her property.

58

No one was more surprised at the way the battle went than were Ywain and Gawain themselves. Neither had ever before met a knight who could match him in fair single combat. Ywain remembered how he and Gawain had borne all before them at tournaments, and he knew he had never met a knight as skillful as this. In like manner, Gawain thought that his old comrade Ywain would be astounded to hear that he, Gawain, had met his match! Yet neither thought for a moment who it might be he was fighting against. And so they fought on the whole day long until the sun began to go down. Gawain's strength was nearly gone, and Ywain knew he could not stand much longer.

"Sir knight," said Ywain, "it grows dark. I do not think any man will reproach us if we call a halt to this fight. Never before have I met any man who has given me such strokes as you have done."

Gawain, who could not recognize his friend's voice—both were too tired to sound like themselves—answered, "Fair sir, I think I have had the worst of it, for you have well repaid all my strokes."

"Tell me, sir," said Ywain then, "what your name is, if you will, for I have never met a better knight than you."

"I am called Gawain, son of King Lot."

When Ywain heard that, he was horrified. He threw his sword on the ground and jumped down from his horse, crying, "Alas, if I had known that there would have been no battle today!"

"Why, who are you then?" asked Sir Gawain.

"Sir," he said, "I am Ywain, who honors you above all other men. Therefore I will do what I can and grant you this battle. You have overcome me by your strength at arms."

60

Sir Gawain answered courteously, "Nay, certainly you have won the day, and I surrender to you, Sir Ywain."

Now the two knights embraced in friendly fashion, delighted to see each other again. What a sight that was for the king and the court! All day long the two had tried to injure each other in bitter battle, and now they were embracing each other like brothers! Everyone watched in silent amazement as the two turned and came back to stand together before the king.

King Arthur looked from one to the other, and said, "I feared that you two would kill each other, and now it appears that you are friends. What has caused such a change?"

"Sire," said Gawain, "there is indeed a quarrel between us still. This knight has conquered me in fair fight, and he will not admit that I am defeated."

"Not so," said Ywain, "for you can all see that I have been defeated by this good knight."

At this everyone was even more confused. Far from claiming to have won the fight, each knight wanted the king to agree he was the loser. Finally Gawain took off his helm and said, "Sire, I am your nephew Gawain, and this is my dear friend Sir Ywain. Never would we two have fought each other if either had known who the other was. I know that if we had fought any longer I would certainly have been slain."

Ywain protested, "No, it is I who was overcome! Gawain has won the victory."

The king was well pleased with both good knights, and eager to end their debate. "Sir Ywain," he said, "welcome to my court! It is long since we have seen you here. Will you both now agree to accept my judgment?"

The knights gladly agreed to this, and the two sisters came forth
before the king. "Ladies," said the king, "you have heard what
these knights have said. Each has declared himself defeated, so
that neither of you has won her case. Will you agree then to let
me settle the matter?"

The younger sister agreed at once. The elder sister hesitated a
moment, then said, "Sire, you are our king. I hope you will not
cheat me out of my rights."

"You shall have your rights," said King Arthur. "You shall be
lady over all your land, and your sister must honor you as her over-
lord. But she shall hold half the land for her own as long as she
gives you due homage and loyalty."

Thus the king settled the dispute, and the two knights were glad to be disarmed. As they stood there and spoke, the lion, who had burst out of his chamber, came running in search of Ywain, his master. When he saw him, he leaped with joy and rushed toward the midst of the crowd where Sir Ywain stood. Everyone there began to run away for fear of the lion, but Ywain called out and said, "Have no fear. This beast will do you no harm. He is my dear friend, and I am his. I would not part with him for anything." ·

When they saw Ywain and the lion together, everyone knew at last that Ywain was the true Knight of the Lion, of whom they had heard so much. Gawain turned to Ywain and said, "I do not deserve your pardon, Sir Ywain, for I have ill repaid you for your kindness to my family. You helped my sister in her hour of need and risked your life in friendship for me, and now you stand wounded by my hand. I did not dream I was fighting you, and I did not know that you were the Knight of the Lion."

"It is time for you both to rest," said King Arthur. "Come, both of you, and let us tend to your wounds."

But Ywain had no wish to stay at the court. As soon as his wounds were healed, he was restless to be on his way. He still had not made his peace with Laudine; he could not rest until he had won her again.

8: The Guardian of the Spring

FINALLY THE TIME came when Ywain could return to the enchanted spring. He left the court quietly, telling no man that he was leaving, with no comrade except his faithful lion. Laudine, he knew, had no champion to defend the spring. Perhaps if he were to raise a storm she might be forced to make peace with him.

So he came again to that familiar spot. He poured the spring water over the stone. At once such a storm arose that Laudine was afraid the walls of her castle would fall, they were so battered by the winds. In her terror she turned to Lunette, saying, "Oh, what shall I do? My town and my castle will both be lost, for I have no one to defend the spring."

"Madame," said Lunette, "I know no man who can help us, unless it be the knight who rescued me and slew the giant Harpin. He could defend you against any attack. But I know well he has sworn not to stay long in any spot until his lady, who has refused to see him for many a day, shall forgive him and take him back into her grace."

"Can we help him, do you think?" asked Laudine. "I will do whatever you think best if only he will come and guard my spring. So tell me, dear Lunette, what you think we should do."

"I think he would gladly come," said Lunette, "if you would but swear to do all in your power to end the quarrel between him and his lady."

"Gladly I will do that," said Laudine.

"Will you swear this?" asked Lunette.

"With all my heart," Laudine answered.

"Then," said Lunette, "I will go in search of the Knight of the Lion. Remember your promise, my lady, and all will be well."

Lunette rode straight to the spring, for she knew well who had caused that storm. There she found Ywain sitting on the ground with his lion stretched out beside him. As Lunette dismounted from her horse, he jumped up and greeted her joyfully. "Thanks be to God," she said, "that I have found you here! I bring you tidings from my lady, who has sworn to be your friend."

"Does she then know who I am?" asked Ywain.

"No, she does not yet know," said Lunette, "but unless she should break her sworn word, all will be well between you. Come with me now, but do not let her see your face until you have made your peace with her."

66

As they rode back toward the castle gate, word went through the town that the Knight of the Lion had returned, and people ran out on the streets to see him ride by. Cheers went up from every throat, for they thought that here at last was one who could protect the dangerous spring. Laudine heard, and rejoiced that Lunette had found him so quickly. She was ready to receive him graciously when Lunette and the Knight of the Lion came into her hall. There Ywain

67

knelt before his lady, while Lunette said, "My lady Laudine, here is the knight you wished to see. Promise him now, as you have promised me, that you will do everything in your power to see that he is restored to his lady's favor."

Laudine gave her hand to the kneeling knight and bade him rise. "Sir knight," she said, "I promise you that it will give me great happiness if I can see you reunited with the lady you serve."

"And do you swear to him," Lunette asked, "that you will fulfill, as best you can, all promises you have made to him?"

"Certainly," said Laudine. "Sir knight, I shall be your grateful friend from this day on. Now tell me what I can do for you."

Ywain still did not dare speak. Lunette spoke again on his behalf, "Madame, then do as you have promised, and bring him peace with his own dear lady. No one can do that but yourself, for he is your promised husband, Ywain."

Laudine started back. She blushed—but indeed she was not truly angry. "How is this!" she cried. "You have deceived me shamefully. But—I have promised, and I shall keep my word."

Sir Ywain was filled with joy at her words. "My lady," he said, "I know well that I have been in the wrong, but I think I have paid for my misdeeds. Never again, if I can help it, shall I fail you in any way. I will stay here with you and keep the spring safe as long as I live, if you will truly forgive me."

The lady smiled her forgiveness. In truth, she was as happy to have Ywain back as he was happy to regain her favor.

The good news quickly spread throughout the castle that the Knight of the Lion was Sir Ywain. Better still, he was back to stay and would soon be their own lord.

All of the folk of the castle and town rejoiced as they prepared for the wedding of Ywain and Laudine. The sorrows of these two now were over. For the rest of their lives they dwelt in peace, and no one ever dared again to trouble their lands with storms, for the guardian of the spring was a knight whom all men knew to be a great champion. Lunette was honored almost as highly as her lord and lady, and the lion stayed by Ywain's side ever after.

ABOUT THE AUTHOR

Constance Hieatt is particularly qualified to tell the story of *The Knight of the Lion* for young readers. She is a specialist in Old and Middle English and professor of English at St. John's University. Her previous books include a retelling of the legend of *Sir Gawain and the Green Knight* for children, as well as other texts, translations, and scholarly commentaries on medieval literature.

Mrs. Hieatt was born in Boston, Massachusetts, and attended Smith College. She received her A.B. and A.M. degrees from Hunter College, and her Ph.D. from Yale University. She and her husband live in New York City but spend much of their time in England, where their home is part of a remodeled manor house in a village near Oxford.

ABOUT THE ARTIST

Joseph Low was born in Coraopolis, Pennsylvania; he attended schools in Oak Park, Illinois, and studied at the University of Illinois. Finding that he could pursue his own artistic interests by studying independently in museums and libraries, Mr. Low concentrated on the graphic arts; he taught himself the skills that he needed and acquired the necessary tools.

After spending some time at the Art Students League in New York City, Joseph Low taught graphic arts at Indiana University for three years. He is not only an artist but also a printer and publisher, with his own Eden Hill Press.

His work has been exhibited in museums across the United States, in South America, in the Orient, and in Europe. He and his wife live in Connecticut in a house overlooking Long Island Sound and the Norwalk islands, a ten-minute walk from their boat, a midget ocean racer.